BLOSSOMING SOULS

SHORT STORY COMPILATION: A JOURNEY THROUGH CHILDHOOD

AMAN PAARTHIV KRISHNAN

First Published in November 2021

ISBN: 978-93-5472-253-0

BLUEROSE PUBLISHERS

www.bluerosepublishers.com

info@bluerosepublishers.com

+91 8882 898 898

Cover Design:

Zainul Abid

Cover Illustration:

Arunima Anil

Typographic Design:

Ilma Mirza

Illustrators:

Sharath Chandran : Stories 3 , 11

Arunima Anil : Stories 1,2,4-10,12-14

Distributed by: BlueRose, Amazon, Flipkart

"The memories we make in our childhood are the ones that we will carry with us for the rest of our lives"

DEDICATION

To my grandfathers in heaven

To my grandmothers

To my parents

And to my little sister, Aditi

Without whom none of this would have

been possible!

CONTENTS

DEDICATION......v
FOREWORD......ix
INTRODUCTION......xiv
ACKNOWLEDGEMENT......xviii

AUTHOR'S NOTE......xxii

FISH KEEPER......1
UNEXPECTED GIFT......9
MEERA ON THE *CHANGADAM**......15
RYAN LEFT AT HOME......22
NEW BOSS......30
THE BELIEVER......35
HAUNTED HOUSE......39
BROKEN VASE......44
THE EXAMINATION......48
FLOWERS FROM AFAR......53
THE LOST TICKET......57
THE BUSINESS BOY......62
DEATH WISH......66

WHEN THE EARTH WAS
STILL GREEN.. 70

APPENDIX 77
REFERENCES.. 85
AUTHOR BIO..88

FOREWORD

Tales from a Sensitive Teen Heart

When I read the stories by *Aman Paarthiv Krishnan,* the first thing that we notice is his sharp observation skills. *Aman's* passion for reading and dedication for observing his surroundings have served as a strong foundation for his stories. The style of narration is straight and simple. He follows conversation mode to tell his tales and this helps to create a feeling that the reader is also part of the story.

Aman is a ninth grader who will turn 14 this year. The range of subjects he deals with in the stories vary from neatly arranged casual observations from his daily life to thoughts carrying deep philosophical insights. In the opening story '***Life of a Quaranteen***', the teenager tries to present a background of the confined lives most children live during a pandemic. The story '***Fish Keeper***' proves how passionately *Ryan*, the protagonist having a striking resemblance with the author, engages with his hobby of ornamental fish farming. The fear of growing big, which will soon force him to break up from his favourite pastime, is intrinsically woven in the story.

The story '***Meera on the Changadam***' is about how the good deeds of a five-year old girl are mistaken by family and neighbours at first. *Aman* concludes the story with a positive note on how *Meera's* mother realizes her mistake. Interestingly, the same author writes about saving a life with the offer of the job of a robber in the story '***Death Wish***'. *Aman's* balance for weighing goodness is sharp and exemplary. The offer of the job of a robber is placed by *Tony* to *Stephen* when the latter was on the threshold of committing suicide. What is a bigger sin? Taking the God-given life by oneself or holding on even by committing petty robberies? I remembered *Jean Valjean* and *Bishop Myriel*, the characters immortalized by *Victor Hugo*, while reading '***Death Wish***'. *Bishop Myriel* had saved *Jean Valjean* by lying to police about the theft at his place as he very well knew robbery is far virtuous an act than committing suicide because of hunger.

The story '***When Earth was still Green***' shows us how wild the imagination of the author can travel. How the earth was deserted by its inhabitants who had given up to a tiny virus and migrated to *Mars* is portrayed engagingly in the story. It is natural that many of the stories are influenced by the pandemic as the author confesses in the introduction that he had started writing the stories after being confined to the four walls of home, a condition forced upon us by the coronavirus.

Aman has a long road to travel. I am sure he will be reading a lot too along with continuing his writing. The art of storytelling needs to be refined like extracting gold from ores. Reading the classics and fine tuning the craft is the only way for that. If his prediction about human beings migrating to *Mars* will come true soon, maybe some of *Aman's* later works will have readers in the Red Planet too!

Thiruvananthapuram
August 1, 2021

B. Sreejan
Associate Editor
The New Indian Express

INTRODUCTION

LIFE IS VERY MUCH LIKE AN ELEVATOR. It can go straight down, and straight up in a matter of seconds. Why would I, or anyone for that matter, write short stories? Why do a short-story book while there are so many others?

Since the age of five, I have been a bookworm. I would read many books until I couldn't read any more. Until my heart was content, I would read. One day, when I became old enough to write something, just like when a cup overflows when it can't handle any more water, all the events I had seen, all the dreams I ever saw, and my own experiences began to surface in me in the form of a few, rough, short stories, that I would write in a diary given to me by my father, and once I was done, I would give it to my mother for reading. She would always say that these stories were quite good enough to be written by a school student, and I would be happy.

I had started reading in 2012, starting with children's magazines and newspapers, and I slowly started reading bigger books as I grew up. I began with moral stories, superhero stories and then I began reading bigger books, full-length novels, such as Harry Potter, The Diary of a Wimpy Kid, Alice in wonderland, which fueled my imagination even more, which reflected when I started writing short stories for the first time.

Having travelled to many places since I was three years old, as a result of my father or mother moving from one place to another, also gave me multiple perspectives of life, which helped me in my writing.

I have written a few real incidents that I faced, while others are pure imagination, and others are experiences of people I've come to know either through my friends, or my family.

However, it was in 2021, during the coronavirus-caused lockdown, that all of the books I had read yielded a great benefit, because, just like how carbon, under pressure, turns into a diamond, my imagination, under the pressure of the lockdown and everything that happened during it, resulted in me creating a lot of short stories!

*Maya Angelou said it best: "**There is no greater agony than bearing an untold story inside you.**"*

Once I got an idea, I would act on it immediately, for later it seemed unappealing to me. When I would act on an idea, the words, the emotion, the story itself would flow automatically out of me, like a waterfall. Sadly, the first of my stories got forgotten, written in random papers, and ultimately, lost.

However, I began writing even more stories, and the more I read, the more I wrote, and I read so much that even a word, a gesture, a smile, a frown, an image, stimulated me so that my mind became an ocean of ideas. I brought a few of these ideas together, I ripped a few and pasted them somewhere else, and now, in the form of these short stories, it waits, to be read by you, to help you see wonderful and sad moments, alike.

Aman Paarthiv Krishnan

August 2021

ACKNOWLEDGEMENT

It is my pleasure to acknowledge the contributions of the people who made this book a reality.

There are many ways in which God has blessed us, and among them, the most important blessing is our parents. We owe our parents the best at all times. To all the parents around the world, this book is a huge thank you!! I'm truly blessed to have such wonderful parents!! Thank you, mom and dad!

Both of them read early drafts and offered advice for the stories, all while making sure that I wouldn't face any problems while I wrote. They were as important to the completion of this book as I was. I owe you everything I have and every part of who I am. Thank you so much, my two lifelines.

Not just genes, but I inherited some valuable and wonderful books too from my late grandfather Mr V Krishnan. Thank you so much!!!

It is impossible to imagine a family without cousins, uncles, aunts, grandparents, or other members of the extended family. The book is also dedicated to my grandparents, cousins Amira and Ivaan, Risa, Kallu, my uncles and aunts, Leji, Kishor Kumar, Rajendran and Salini. Without the contributions of each of these individuals, none of these stories would exist.

I express my sincere gratitude to my Guru, Mentor, Yamini Ma'am, who spent time in order to go through the manuscript during her busy schedule.

I am thankful to Miss Shreya and her professional feedback on the manuscript. Thanks to her for her speedy response.

A special thanks to everyone at Blue Rose Publications, including my consultants Arjun and Sanya, Bhanupriya, my publication manager.

To my illustrators, Sharathchandran and Arunima Anil, both of whose artworks have helped bring life to my stories.

A big thanks to Mr B Sreejan, the Associate Editor, The New Indian Express, who has beautified these stories with his wonderful foreword!

Finally, a big thank you to Dr Shashi Tharoor, who served as my inspiration for writing this book, and offered an honest appreciation for it!!

BLOSSOMING SOULS

AUTHOR'S NOTE: LIFE OF A QUARANTEEN:

"In the dark times will there also be singing? Yes, there will also be singing. About the dark times."
— ***Bertolt Brecht***

AS A RESULT OF A RARE CATASTROPHE, the Coronavirus pandemic, a tragically large number of human lives have been lost. To contain the pandemic, countries include quarantines and social distancing practices. We have never seen a collapse in activity like this in our lifetimes. As a result, there is significant uncertainty about the impact of the crisis on people's lives and livelihoods.

All of it began in 2019, when a Chinese man from Wuhan went to the Huanan market in Wuhan, according to news channels. Yet unexpectedly, he was taken to a hospital with a supposed fever a few hours after he went home (1,2).

Only later was it discovered that he had a mutant version of SARS-CoV, the 2003 strain of a virus, that would completely hit the reset button on the world (3).

Bats, snakes and pangolins had been cited as potential carriers based on the genetic sequence isolated from these animals and the DNA of the virus isolated from SARS-CoV-2 infected patients (4-6).

Fast Forward to 2021- millions of lives have been lost, nations have been in lockdown, many have been hospitalized, even a small fever scare everyone.

There have been survivors, major cities have been pollution-free (7,8), and somehow, life is going on. We all have been through grief, anger, pain, but, looking at the bright side, at the same time, there has been positivity.

Most of us have been able to move on, catch up with family and friends, explore our roots, try many hobbies, discover our inner talents, and so on. It almost feels as if God has hit the reset button, trying to tell us to move on, and try to replace negativity with positivity.

As said before, millions of lives have been lost, but from a certain point of view, God has embraced them. He has helped them to be with us anytime, anywhere.

Schools have been closed, we got online classes. Jobs were lost, entrepreneurship sprouted. Junk food chains were closed, we began to make healthy, homemade food. Sometimes, that is what life is all about! Replacing negativity with positivity!!!

****

FISH KEEPER

"Aquariums tell stories that everyone interprets differently."–***Anonymous***

RYAN REALIZED, TO HIS HORROR, on the way back to their home in the city, that he had forgotten to pack his fish.

When Ryan informed his mother of this, she instructed him, in a calm demeanour, to never repeat his actions again, and how if he would not change his habits, something even worse might happen. She also felt a bit of pity on him, for everyone in the car knew he was never going to own a pet again.

Back at Ryan's mother's home, both Ivaan and Amy were playing with Ryan's prized pet, his turtle. She knew Ryan would be taking his final exams the next day, and that he would be promoted to 9th grade, which is an important milestone in any teen's life. As a result, Ryan's mother would never allow him to own a pet again, meaning Amy would own it all for more than two years.

Amy thought that she would tell Ryan when he called the next time. She was feeling ecstatic at the fact that she had acquired almost 300 fishes and a turtle, while Ivaan, being a one-year-old, was simply more than happy to play with the turtle.

****

Ryan loved to keep fish. He got his first school of fish from a generous neighbour, who seemed to have many species, divided by kind, in separate tanks.

He was also an expert in various things, like managing his pet fishes, fixing any issue someone has with their phone, and he also had a knack for fixing things easily, with the touch of his hand. However, he was quite a bit inconsistent with his studies, despite being a bit of an expert in everything else.

After a few months, and a few deaths of his fish along the way, Ryan became an experienced fish-keeper, and knew how, and which ones were to breed, and had hundreds of them himself, some of which he sold to his neighbours, for almost reasonable prices.

One day, his mother announced that they all had to go to her village, due to some emergency. His father was going out-of-station for a few weeks. As for Ryan's classes, it was online.

When they started packing, Ryan was not a bit anxious about the fish. But his mother, who always floccinaucinihilipilified them, became concerned, asking questions, like:

"How are you going to bring your fish? What are you going to do if something happens to them?" and the like.

Ryan was a bit annoyed by his mother's sudden concern for his fish. All of them got in a rush to pack all essentials.

Ryan transferred a quarter of his fish into a bucket, and he had almost 1000 in total. He handed over the rest to his neighbours, divided as fractions.

In the car, the fish and its necessities became a bane, for it occupied too much space, due to which Ryan also obtained a few imprecations to his face.

On the way, Ryan and his sister Lisa were remarkably quiet. The only occasions when both sister and brother were so quiet and actually behaved like brother and sister were when both of them were playing a game on their device, or if they were asleep, or if they had unintentionally caused an issue in the car, and got scolded.

Ryan's mother was watching them through the mirror and noticed both of them taking turns to give food to the fish, which they were doing with very much coordination.

At Ryan's mother's place, there were 4 people at that time. His aunt, his cousins, Ivaan, a 10-month-old, and Amy, who was 8 years of age, and his grandmother.

When they finally reached his maternal place, some from his collection of fish had died. Nevertheless, Ryan did not mind as the others were fine.

His cousins were completely exhilarated about the shoal of fish. If Ivaan was not to be seen, one only had to go near the fish tank, where both Amy and Ivaan would be playing with the turtle, Ryan's prized possession.

Every weekend, it was a hassle for Ryan and his cousin, Amy. She was inclined only to play with the fish, and the wage for helping Ryan was one guppy per job. It was not much, but it brought a smile to her face.

On the day Ryan was to leave, everyone got in a hurry to pack everything. Ryan's grandmother had made some pickles, wrapped some food in banana leaves, but there was not enough space with all the other things, taking in mind the fish.

However, Amy had proposed to watch a movie on that day, and of course, Ryan kept his promise (How could he not!) and watched a horror movie with Lisa and Amy.

After watching the movie, there was not much of any work to help with, but they did what they were told. After a quick lunch, they all left for their hometown.

Obviously, without his pet fish!!!

When they were halfway to their hometown, Ryan realized that they never took the bucket of fish from their mother's house.

After four full minutes of loud laughing, his mother yelled "Good Riddance", and advised him. While back at Ryan's mother's place, Amy could not stop grinning, at the fact that she was now the proud owner of a shoal of fish and a turtle.

****

UNEXPECTED GIFT

"Sometimes unexpected gifts give you that happiness which is worth more than expected gifts and surprises" – ***Unknown***

RYAN WISHED THAT HE WOULD GET A PHONE. His 12th birthday was nearing, and he already had a lot of old presents, such as a base model phone, a variety of costly pens, various storybooks, remote control cars, and the like.

He quietly went to his parents' bedroom and waited till his parents stopped quarrelling. He entered the room, and his parents looked at him in anger.

His sister, Lisa, exclaimed, "Your birthday is going to be held at mom's house in the village!" Ryan stood stunned.

His parents would usually celebrate birthdays at expensive restaurants, with different flavours of cake each time. This was an unexpected change!

Nevertheless, Ryan quietly aired his demand.

"A Phone!" exclaimed Ryan's mother furiously. "Look at how your pampering has spoiled him!" his mother said to his father.

"We are planning to make your 12th birthday a little bit more humble, dear son, to teach you values such as humility and discipline." said his father, in a calm voice.

Ryan went back to his room, and anyone could feel the melancholy radiating from him.

Two days before his birthday, everyone started packing their bags, and Ryan did some extra packing for his fish.

His father had to be out-of-station and so would be joining Ryan's birthday via video call.

On reaching maternal home, his cousin Amy greeted them cheerfully, but Ryan seemed to be more concerned about his fish, which he had accidentally left out last time, than about his own birthday.

Over the days, they planned which of Amy's friends should be invited because Amy's little brother Ivaan also had the same birthday as Ryan. Other preparations were also there, regarding the flavour of the cake, types of food items to be served, decorations etc.

Meanwhile, Ryan was appointed as Ivaan's babysitter. If not occupied with Ivaan, he would be doing his summer vacation homework.

One day, while playing with Ivaan, Ryan saw his cousin Amy, playing with something that appeared to be a........'An iPhone'?!

Ryan quickly handed Ivaan to Amy and almost ripped away the gadget from Amy's hands. He checked it carefully and exclaimed, "My God, It's a real iPhone!" He pressed the power button, at which a battery icon flashed.

Soon he ran to his mom's room and put the phone for charging, and immediately contacted his uncle to ask about the phone.

According to his uncle's narrative, during his days of working at a resort in the Middle East, the phone had arrived through the laundry, as told by his friend.

After waiting for several days, since nobody came to claim it, he came to his native place later that year and handed it to his daughter Amy as a plaything. Ryan's uncle instructed him to sneak it out without letting his cousin know.

It was on full charge now. Ryan took a safety pin and checked the sim tray. No sim card at all. He did not care. Ivaan was quietly watching everything unfold and quickly ran back to Amy as if he was trying to speak.

After the birthday celebration, everyone left. Ryan and his mother quickly got to packing because Ryan's father said he was going to return the day after tomorrow. This time, Ryan was prepared. He packed his fish into the car and then packed everything else.

After a quick lunch, they began to leave. At the last minute, Ryan realised he had forgotten to bring his smartwatch, and so went back to get it. Getting into the car after getting his watch, Ryan double-checked, wondering if he had forgotten something.

This time, something more precious belonging to Ryan had been lost: Ryan's Maths textbook. This realisation hit Ryan when his mother stopped for tea. Coincidentally, Amy also began to call Ryan to tell him about the textbook.

Ryan was playing music from his new iPhone, and chose to keep quiet about the textbook. Meanwhile, back at his mother's home, Amy was attempting to read Ryan's Math textbook with a puzzled expression on her face!!

****

MEERA ON THE *CHANGADAM**

*"There is more to life than just increasing its speed." – **Mahatma Gandhi***

EVERYONE IN THE NEIGHBOURHOOD WAS EXTREMELY worried about their children. Meera was the cause of it all. Everyone went over to her house, and started scolding her parents.

Meera's mother grew very concerned when the neighbours started approaching her. She stood there, completely embarrassed, and decided that Meera was going to sleep without having dinner.

In the middle of the ruckus, a boy came and said "Why are you all scolding Meera's mother? Didn't anyone inform you all? Meera and her friends saved a drowning lady!"

Everyone was stunned, and in complete silence for a minute. The boy instructed everyone to come with him.

*****

******Changadam (Barge)*: is a shoal-draft flat-bottomed boat, built mainly for river and canal transport of bulk goods. Barges are made up of banana stem, logs, bamboos etc. Barges have changed through time.

Meera was naughtier than an average 5-year-old. She wanted to poke her head into whatever was going on nearby. Being a girl, she could, and would taunt her rivals by claiming that they scolded her or beat her, even if they did not.

There was nothing in the world she did not want to try out or play with. Whenever she wanted a guava fruit or a berry to eat, she would just climb the tree at that very moment without even seeking help from any elders.

Every time it started to rain, Meera would go out and receive a beating or two for playing in the rain.

One monsoon day, it had been raining very heavily, so Meera's neighbour, Matthews made a changadam (barge) and ferried people from one side to another. Meera saw all this unfold. She quickly got out with an umbrella; in case it might rain.

Meera asked the neighbour if she could accompany him, and her neighbour agreed. They went from house to house, offering home delivery, and every child saw Meera travelling on a ferry.

After going to the houses, the changadam was full of children, and groceries. After delivering the groceries, Matthews took the children to a nearby lake, where one could catch a lot of fish by using a towel or a cover.

Meera and the other children started playing in the rain, while Matthews caught fish for the children. After half an hour, the rain stopped, but there was still a lot of water, and so, everyone went back on the changadam.

On their way back to homes, the children were singing merrily, when Meera spotted someone drowning in the floodwater! "Stop! Stop! Look there! Someone is drowning!" Meera shouted aloud.

All the children stopped their activities, and Matthews quickly turned the boat around. All of them quickly helped the person get onto the boat. The children saw that it was their teacher!

They woke her up, and stopped nearby, where other people were waiting to help. Some people gathered around the teacher, and a doctor who stayed nearby attended to her.

When she woke up, she described the day's events from her perspective:

In the morning, about an hour before the flood, she was going to the school to pick up a few things she had forgotten, and so was travelling on her scooter, and that when she got to the place where she was found, she could not distinguish the floodwater from the road, and rode into the water.

Meanwhile, Meera and the other children, along with Matthews were congratulated, and were given garlands!!!

Back home, Meera's mother got to know what had happened from all the neighbours, and was waiting outside with a cane in her hand.

Meera went up to her mother, wearing the garland and clutching the fish she caught from the lake, and proudly described the day's events without any regret, how she adventured on the changadam, how she played with the other children, and how she saved her teacher.

Holding the cane in her hands, Meera's mother decided not to punish her. She instead kissed Meera on the cheeks and advised her a great deal about the accidents that happened during the rain, and provided her with a delicious dinner.

****

RYAN LEFT AT HOME

"Loneliness might be taking you towards an otherwise unreachable experience of reality" -
Olivia Laing

THE POWER CONNECTION FAILED HALF AN HOUR AGO. Ryan was crying when his neighbours arrived. By that time, the power was back on again. They tried to offer him comforting words, and offered him plenty of food items, but Ryan, even though relieved, did not open the door out of fear.

Ryan talked to all the aunties and uncles outside his door about what had happened. A few minutes later, everyone saw Ryan's mother come up the stairs. Seeing the crowd, Ryan's mother became afraid whether something had happened to her son.

*****

Ryan's father worked for an NGO. Recently, they had got a project in the national capital. Therefore, Ryan's father had gotten transferred to New Delhi.

Ryan's small family, including his mother and father, shifted completely to Delhi, which was an entirely new place for a 5-year-old Ryan and his family.

Even though his father had been transferred to New Delhi, Ryan's father had to shuttle between Delhi and Kerala. Once, his father had to go to Kerala for a two-month-long job. Ryan and his mother were all alone in the flat during that time.

When his father was in Delhi, they used to go shopping every weekend at INA market, where they could get any South Indian food items. Ryan's father loved to have traditional home-cooked Kerala food all the time. But he and his mother were fond of fast and instant food like noodles, sandwiches, non-veg dishes etc.

Since Delhi was such a place of various food items, both of them were more than happy to be there.

And hence they never wasted a chance to experience different kinds of food. Whenever his father was out of town, they would plan to enjoy such food items.

Just like any other 5-year-old, Ryan liked to go to various places with his mother. At 7:00 PM daily, an Aloo-Tikki seller used to visit Ryan's housing complex with his hand-cart. The Seller's son would come every day with his father to help him in serving plates to the customers.

If father is not at home, instead of making an elaborate dinner, Ryan and his mother would rather wait for the Aloo-Tikki seller, to have their favourite food, and the seller was also happy to be accustomed to sell there for his frequent customers.

At other times, Ryan and his mother would go together to the roadside shops at Gole Market and have various dishes such as noodles, sandwiches, golgappas and the like.

One day, Ryan came to know from a television advertisement that his favourite superhero movie was to be shown the day after tomorrow. From that day, he started counting back to the day when his favourite movie would come on TV.

When the day that Ryan's favourite movie would get broadcast arrived, Ryan's father called and informed them that he was going to arrive within a few hours to pick up a few things and then would immediately go to Mumbai.

Ryan's mother was shocked to hear this. He never arrived unannounced. Ryan's mother quickly dressed up in order to go shopping, because there was nothing left for cooking some additional meals.

When she asked Ryan whether he wanted to come along, Ryan said he did not want to leave watching the movie, and his mother decided it was better to leave him alone because he caused a lot of trouble.

While they were in the middle of the road, his shoes would get unbuckled. When they were in the shop, Ryan would pick up a bag of potato chips and start eating them even before making the payment.

Taking this in mind, Ryan's mother gave her phone to Ryan, thinking that in case there was a power failure and if the TV gets turned off, he can be engaged with the phone without the thought that he is alone at home. Then, she left for shopping.

Just after she left, a very scary sequence was going on in the movie, and the power connection went out all of a sudden.

Ryan's mother's phone started ringing on full volume!! Moreover, it was a very frightening ringtone, and it made Ryan think of ghosts.

Ryan picked up the call. It was his father. "Hello, hello? Ryan? Where is your mother?!" He began asking Ryan. Ryan started sobbing.

His father asked him what happened and asked him to give the phone to his mother. Ryan was very much tensed and could utter only the words "Mom-mom...."

His father had just got inside the flight, and for one second, he did not know what to do at that moment. A few seconds passed. He could only hear the sound of Ryan crying over the phone

Ryan's father became scared, and immediately called all of his neighbours. Everyone was out for weekend shopping for essentials, but got scared for their neighbour's child.

They dropped their shopping and immediately went there. By the time all the neighbours had arrived, the power had come back on, and when Ryan's mother arrived, she found all of them comforting Ryan.

When they saw her coming, immediately all of them started scolding her for leaving the child alone, and for disrupting their weekend shopping.

Ryan's mother was completely embarrassed, and apologized to everyone for her mistake. After everything was said and done, Ryan's mother was done making dinner, and she heard a knock on the door.

Ryan's mother readied herself again to receive a heavy load of imprecations from her husband!!!

****

NEW BOSS

"Show respect to people that don't deserve it; Not as a reflection of their character, but as a reflection of yours" – ***Dave Willis***

IT HAD BEEN A FINE MORNING, but not for the employees of 'Bio-Graphics'. It was an extremely wonderful day for them!!! Everyone got to know the news from Shankar, who liked to arrive early in the morning.

The Boss was retiring. The old man was 65, a nagging but cromulent fellow, who would start screaming if any of his employees committed even a spelling mistake.

Mr. Mathew Wilson must have been an Army commander in his past birth, for he would have screamed at his employees for even the smallest mistakes they had made.

Shankar went home at 5:00 P.M, which was when his shift ended. He was a biker.

Shankar was not one bit superstitious as his mother and his late friend, Joshua Lewis, were. They would always tell him something, such as "You shouldn't go there on that day", "You shouldn't do this after a specific time", and so on.

Shankar never believed any of it, but it all came true, and luckily, it would happen at least not in front of his friend or his mother.

A few weeks later, Shankar was speeding off to his office since he was late. All of a sudden, a black cat crossed his road. Shankar remembered his friend, Joshua's advice.

Not minding any of that, he went on his way carelessly, when he accidentally brushed a car's mirror. The man inside lowered his window, and Shankar readied himself to give and receive imprecations.

Some people stopped by, both because it was the usual office time at every office, and to watch the exchange of curses; it was like watching a snake-and-mongoose fight.

After fifteen full minutes of word war, Shankar drove off to his office, ignoring the curses still pouring out of the man's mouth.

He reached office, where everyone was busy seen decorating everything. His friend at work, Vikram, handed him a few balloons and asked him to blow them.

When asked as to why the entire office was being decorated, the response came quick. "Didn't you hear the news? The new boss is arriving today, which is why everyone is busy with the decorations."

30 minutes later, the old door creaked. The man Shankar had fought with just about 40 minutes earlier walked in. Shankar realized that he should have heeded Joshua's words when he had once said that a black cat crossing one's path brought bad luck.

The man whose car Shankar had hit, was his new boss, Mr. George. He saw Shankar across the crowd, and gave him the 'I will deal with you later' look.

****

THE BELIEVER

"A superstition is a premature explanation that overstays its time." – ***George Iles***

EVERYWHERE THAT JOSHUA LOOKED, there was floodwater. From the eighth floor, he could see the homes in the nearby slum getting flooded.

His phone was repeatedly vibrating from all the messages from people who cared about him, messages about heavy rain and flash flood in the state where Joshua was vacationing. He was extremely worried about the situation.

Joshua Lewis was a superstitious man. At the age of thirty-six, people would expect a man to be quite sensible and smart, but Joshua was absolutely a nervous wreck.

He always did anything that had even little or no importance, only after checking with his astrologer. He would first check the 'zodiac sign' and 'this and that sign' of people even when making new friends.

On a rather curious occasion, when his friends decided to go to India, Joshua tagged along merrily, without checking with his astrologer, which was why it was curious. He vacationed there for half a month, but unexpectedly, a flash flood warning arrived.

The entire locality, even the entire city where Joshua was vacationing got flooded. The hotel where Joshua and his friends were staying also got flooded, and Joshua, being the extreme fanatic that he was, helped everything in any way but refused to be helped.

"God will save me, all of you leave this place!" was the response. A lot of boats passed, but Joshua drove them off, claiming that God will save him.

After a while, even after being an 'expert swimmer', Joshua found himself on the bridge between Heaven, Earth, and Hell.

Joshua found God, standing with an angry look on his face. Joshua asked God," God, why did you not help me, despite all the devotion I have shown to you"?

"You fool, I sent several boats by your way, I also asked through your friends if you wanted to save yourself, but you never wanted to be saved!"

The next day, Joshua's body was taken home. During his funeral, his friends recounted his bravery, how he refused to be helped and how superstitious he was, as his soul watched everything in anguish.

****

HAUNTED HOUSE

During the day, I don't believe in ghosts. At night, I'm a little open-minded." – ***Anonymous***

WILL WAS HANGING OUT WITH HIS FRIENDS AFTER School, and it was 3 P.M, and all of them were in the bus stand near the school, waiting for a bus to appear while playing 'Truth or Dare'.

If it was 'truth', it was either 'Tell us this or that' and if it was 'dare', it would be 'Go and do this to so-and-so'.

All of them stayed in the same neighbourhood, and taking this in mind, one of his friends from him dared him to "Go and stay in the 'Haunted House', at the corner of the street".

Will's throat went dry at the mention of the scary building, from where loud wails came, and he started to feel as if he was shrinking within. When someone offered to keep him company, he reluctantly agreed.

His parents were going to be away for the week, and had trusted him with his elder sister and brother, and also had asked their next-door neighbours to keep a check on the three.

Will, at his house, packed up a few necessities into a bag, such as his phone and his flashlight, and his friend who volunteered to accompany him came.

His brother teased him, asking, "Where are you going to, the orphanage?". Will talked about a sleepover at Andy's, the friend who was going to accompany him. His elder sister grew a little suspicious but let him go anyway.

They cycled to the Haunted House, which was half a mile away. When they got inside, it looked as if they were at a hotel for spiders, because the entrance itself was full of cobwebs.

His friend, Andy, lit a candle, and took the webs off, remarking, "Oh Lord, anyone could have made a full wedding gown out of these!".

Meanwhile, Will was examining the decades-old furniture, the massive library, and he wondered how exquisite the entire house would look if it were cleaned.

Will and Andy clicked pictures of themselves at the haunted house, to show them off to their friends. They also started to take whichever books they liked, considering that since the entire house was in an abandoned state, no-one would ever bother about the books.

They ventured out to see if there was anything else they could take home. Will found a watch, while Andy found branded sunglasses and game CDs.

All of a sudden, from far inside the haunted house, which they were planning to make their clubhouse, they heard a loud noise, and a sound which seemed like a dog's wail.

Will shivered frantically, and so did Andy. He tried to take the torch. He quickly turned it on, and when he turned it on, it perfectly aligned with all the mirrors in the house, so that the entire house lit up.

He hoped that no one would notice the lights, and started to pray that some 40-foot-tall, 100-pound monster would not pop its head out.

Will heard some kind of movement. A tiny creature appeared from inside a bedroom.

A puppy!!! A puppy was the cause of all of this sham, all this time! “So, what are we going to do about this ‘little monster’?” After laughing a lot, Andy asked.

“Seeing that there is no other way, I’ll adopt him.” Will answered, while giving the puppy a biscuit.

****

BROKEN VASE

"Trust is like a vase...Once it's broken, though you can fix it, the vase will never be the same again. – ***Walter Inglis Anderson***

ANDY WAS EATING HIS SHAWARMA IN THE BACK OF THE car, with the joy of knowing that the summer vacation had begun. His father himself came to pick Andy up, and right after reaching the nearest Shawarma joint, they bought Milk Shake and a Shawarma roll, for each of them.

After reaching home, his parents said that they had some urgent business, and were leaving Andy with his little siblings for a few hours.

Before leaving, they told Andy things such as "Do not watch TV", "Do not go out to play", "Revise your lessons" and "Watch out for your siblings".

Once they left, he started watching TV, despite being told not to do so. While he was watching some superhero movie, a loud shattering noise reached his ears.

Andy did not immediately become concerned about it, but after some time, he became anxious. The sound seemed to have come from his parents' bedroom.

At the door, he stepped on something very sharp. He looked at his bleeding foot, and inspected the object that had cut through his skin.

The object looked strange, like a shard of glass.

The siblings stood near, trying to look as innocent as kittens. Andy rushed to get the first-aid kit from the medicine cabinet in the kitchen and nursed his foot.

As he inspected the debris of the broken object, he realised that it was from the broken flower vase.

It was bought by his father for his mother, on her birthday. That was almost three years ago, but it seemed precious, nevertheless. He washed his foot and quickly got to clearing the mess, alongside his siblings.

Two hours later, when his parents came back, they were looking really happy. They did not seem to mind the fact that the TV was on.

Apparently, they had gone to see an astrologer, who told them that something auspicious was on its way, but something unlucky would be lost.

They then noticed Andy's bandages, to which he replied that he had gone outside to play and then cut himself. Andy denied breaking the vase when they noticed the vase had gone missing.

“Ah!” his parents exclaimed. The divine one has come and taken it for himself! Something really good is on its way! Anyhow, we found that thing completely useless."

****

THE EXAMINATION

*"Success isn't always about greatness. It's about consistency. Consistent hard work leads to success. Greatness will come." -**Dwayne Johnson***

RAJIV WAS NEARING THE END OF THE SCHOOL YEAR. He was an average student, inconsistent with his marks, sometimes a class topper, or below average. This time, Rajiv was determined to be the Class Topper in every subject.

He had passed tenth grade with distinction, because of which his parents had bought him a smartphone which caused him to become a bit arrogant and over-confident over time. This was the reason why he stooped to an average level.

Even when the final exams were announced, Rajiv casually said “Yes” and went to his bedroom, and played games on his phone.

When there was only one more week for the final exam, he immediately quit all other activities and started studying. The first subject on the timetable was Business studies, then accountancy, then math and the rest.

On the day of the exam, Rajiv’s father dropped him at the venue. Rajiv was confident that he would pass the final exam in flying colors.

The question paper arrived. He read the first question. What is meant by 'accounting cycle'?

Accountancy!!!!!!!

But it was supposed to be ‘Business Studies’.

Rajiv’s hand shot to the sky like an arrow. The invigilator was a Physical Education teacher, known for his cromulent, ruthless sarcasm. He glowered at him. “Ask your question aloud”.

“Sir, according to the Time table, it is supposed to be ‘Business Studies’ today, but this is ‘Accountancy’ question paper!” Rajiv asked his question.

“Ha! Seems, like all other nitwits, you did not notice the revised time-table, is it, Rajiv?” The teacher asked. Rajiv sat down in his seat and shivered uncontrollably. He scrawled down everything he knew.

His parents had promised him a MacBook if he could score well. Rajiv wrote everything he knew on the answer paper. A few weeks later, the result declaration came.

Rajiv had perfectly passed in everything except, of course, Accountancy; in fact, he had only got through, somehow. Rajiv's parents gave him the "No dinner for you, you loser!" look, and Rajiv went back to his room.

Rajiv's sister, in her room, was singing in a cruel, sing-song voice: "Once an Average, Always an Average!"

****

FLOWERS FROM AFAR

"There are flowers in my chest again, the kind that do not lose their bloom." - ***Rumi***

"Every flower is a soul blossoming in nature"

ON A WARMING SUNNY DAY, a beautiful Marigold stood blooming, showing off its unchallenged beauty, as if it was standing on top of the other flowers.

That was until it got plucked along with the others, and then, it got loaded on a truck with its former neighbours. Later, it was bought by a bouquet-maker, who made flower bouquets for all kinds of occasions.

From there, as a funeral - bouquet, it was sold to an old bank manager. It was bought for a late friend of his, who died the other day. He was his best friend ever since they met, and his late friend of his had held the position before he did.

After the funeral was held, the bouquets were buried in the garden.

Several years later, what a surprise!!! In the same garden, a majestic marigold became the nesting ground for butterflies, who were going to morph from caterpillars to adults!!

Watching the children of the house play, until they were called indoors, it looked very beautiful in its simplicity!!

Watching the birds, the beautiful sunsets, and the beautiful kids who would live there for years to come, it spent the rest of its life in the same way!!!

****

THE LOST TICKET

"Well, you can't win the lottery, if you don't have a ticket." – ***Andy Gray***

TO RAMAN, buying a lot of lottery tickets were the same as alcohol to an alcoholic. When he went up to the Lottery-Seller each month-end, with some of his monthly salary, the seller would smile, asking every time.

"Why do you toil each month and waste your money here? Use it judiciously for something better. Do you know that it is a million to one fluke?" The lottery seller would ask.

"I do it for my family so that they could live in a mansion, like royals, buy them whatever they want." was the reply, every time.

Sometimes, when luck was on his side, he would win a few thousand rupees, then he would give it to his wife.

Today also, he was confident of winning the first prize and was determined only to think of positive results. He had bought 10 tickets just to be sure.

When the paper-boy brought the newspaper the next day, Raman woke up even earlier than the rooster and checked the newspaper immediately. By this time, everyone else had been woken up by Raman's preparation for the grand results.

He checked the page on which the lottery results came, and ignored the brickbats his mother and wife were throwing for waking them up unnecessarily. He looked up his own ticket numbers. One of his tickets had won 5000.

But there was one last ticket left.

Where had it gone?

Raman racked his brains. All of a sudden, he was not able to remember where he had kept the last ticket.

He ordered his children around and instructed them to find the last ticket. It could turn out to be their ticket to royalty.

Then-10-month-old Sivani, the youngest child of the family, began speaking for the first time.

Seeing the spectacle themselves, everyone rushed to the bedroom, hoping to hear the baby say their name.

"P-p" the baby started. "Parvathy! Hello, Parvathy! He's trying to say my name, said the eldest of the three children.

"No, she's attempting to say my name! Pallav! Pallav!" claimed the middle child.

"P-Pillow!!!" the baby shouted. Everyone was disappointed, because the first words of a baby were what, or who, the baby liked.

Parvathy, meanwhile, was examining the pillow, as to why it would be a baby's first word. She became exhilarated.

"Father, Sivani has found the ticket!! Baby Sivani has found the ticket" Parvathy screamed. Raman ran to the bedroom, where he found the ticket lying under the baby's pillow.

Raman ran back to the newspaper with the lottery ticket and checked the winners' list again. He could not believe his eyes, neither could his mother, nor his wife.

They had won more than a crore!

Raman quickly dressed up in his best attire and caught a bus to the place where the winners were to claim their prizes.

10 years later, a 10-year-old Sivani asked her mother to recount how they had won a crore, while Parvathy and Pallav were watching a movie on their computer.

Raman was at his travel agency, which he named Rajeshwara Travel Agency, counting the day's earnings. He began to wonder. "I guess it's time to buy one more lottery ticket!" he said aloud.

****

THE BUSINESS BOY

"Sell a man a fish, he eats for a day, teach a man how to fish, you ruin a wonderful business opportunity."
– ***Karl Marx***

MADHAV WAS A 10-YEAR-OLD, but he was running a business by himself. Now, it wasn't the kind of businesses run by big people in tuxedos, but Madhav could earn 150 rupees in 3 days with his fish business.

Madhav had his own fish stall, and he was the only pet-fish seller in his place who offered home delivery. He also was an experienced fish breeder.

One day, having earned fame in nearby places, Madhav's mother suggested that he advertise his fish business on social media.

Reluctant at first, Madhav created an account for his business, then sent out advertisements.

The next day, at 9:00 A.M exact, someone, apparently a restaurant owner, gave a call on Madhav's mother's phone with an order for 500 guppies.

Madhav's mother was surprised, and when Madhav talked to the caller, he was shocked.

“Five hundred guppies?!

He expects me to sell him Five hundred guppies?!" Madhav asked his mother, shocked.

Madhav was tensed. He usually sold a pair for 30 rupees, and due to lockdown, he would get orders from here and there, and 50 of them would get sold in a week.

Madhav was an expert in estimating the number of fish in each tank. There were almost 100 in each tank according to Madhav, and Madhav had 4 tanks. He thought about stopping his business, because more orders were coming through his phone.

Madhav's older brother, Shashank, gave Madhav a piece of advice: "Why don't you try forming a union of fish keepers? That way, a lot of your friends will be able to know more about business, along with learning from their textbooks!"

Something exploded in Madhav's mind. He quickly rang up all the people he knew who were fish keepers, and told them about the orders. Most of them agreed to co-operate, but some declined, saying they had to study a lot, and others simply said they weren't ready for a big change.

Madhav's friends-turned-co-workers turned the former storeroom outside Madhav's house into a perfect fish shop and brought all the fish to the shop.

Now, according to a new population check, '*Aquaria Co.*', as Madhav and his friends named their new company, had more than 1500 guppies, 300 goldfish, 150 catfish, and several others.

Madhav agreed to each order, and by month-end, 1200 guppies, and 100 goldfish varieties, and 30 catfish varieties were sold.

As for '*Aquaria Co.*', everyone got a lot of profit, and the company had to decline orders for a month, because every volunteer was catching up with the population decrease in their fish tanks!!!

****

DEATH WISH

"Even the best thief in the world can't steal time."
*– **Ally Carter***

STEVEN WILSON COULDN'T ARRIVE AT A CONCLUSION. He was deciding how he would make his grand departure from earth. Copper Sulphate, he had heard, would feel as if your veins were exploding or your stomach was bursting.

Stabbing himself was ruled out, so was lying on the train tracks. Drowning would be better. Just a few minutes of suffocation. That would have been better.

The next day, Steven decided he would rather die with style, and so wore the brand-new shirt his mother had bought him at the gala. He went to the river, but someone else was there prior.

NO

The other person broke the silence. “Come for a bath?” was the question. Steven nodded in silence. Only Steven himself knew the reason.

The other man surmised Steven’s thoughts about coming to the river bank. It wasn’t that he was some kind of a prophet, but only someone depressed to death that he wouldn’t be scared of standing in a river with the water level almost up to the head.

The man thought so and questioned Steven if that was why he had come to the river. Steven was somewhat annoyed but nodded silently.

I am Anthony Jesper, but you can call me Tony" he introduced himself. Have you ever wanted to get a job that pays lots, but in irregular amounts?” The man offered.

The reason Steven was so depressed was that he was not able to get a job. He was in desperate need of work. Now he was a bit confused.

What kind of work would pay irregularly? Surely, this man wasn't talking about - "Well, we're talking about being a robber. Okay, you can either join me in this world or join God."

Steven joined hands without a second thought. Suddenly, having some sort of job was better than not having one at all. He dressed himself up and joined Tony in his misadventures.

****

WHEN THE EARTH WAS STILL GREEN

"I don't think the human race will survive the next thousand years, unless we spread into space."
– ***Stephen Hawking***

THE CLOCK STRUCK MIDNIGHT. Except for Hannah, everyone else was asleep. She got up from her bed and walked to the window.

Workers on Night-Duty oxygenation were working nonstop. Hannah couldn't sleep because she kept thinking about her sister's textbook, which had a chapter about how the planet earth looked centuries ago.

Hannah had mastered the art of being as silent as an ant, and so she got out of her room, went into her elder sister's room, and took the textbook.

She quickly got back to her room and started reading the textbook.

Hannah was only 12 years old, but she had studied everything she could about planet earth.

Her sister was in college, and so, as a part of the syllabus, she had to learn a lot about earth, and everything about evolution, and everything else regarding various kinds of scientific philosophy.

Her sister's textbook had pictures of the earth in the past, a big sphere, almost blue, except for a few patches of green-coloured land!

It also had pictures of big, brown structures with green outgrowths. These were called trees!!

Hannah heard footsteps, and so she immediately turned off the electrical textbook, and tucked it under her pillow, and immediately pulled her blanket on.

She could see who had come from inside the blanket. It was her elder sister.

"So, it seems you like sleepwalking, huh, little sister?"

Her sister broke the silence. "Hand over the textbook. Now." Her sister spoke again.

Hannah quietly pushed the blanket away and handed over the e-textbook.

“So, you wanna know more about how the earth looked like in the past?!!!” asked her sister, looking at the browser history of the e-book.

” Could you tell me everything you know about the past?” Hannah asked honestly.

“Fine, but do not tell Mom and Dad about any of this.” came the answer. “So, you must have read that the earth had a very high population and pollution rate since the beginning of the 21st century?!”

“Yes”!

“So, you might also know why people going to Earth from our home planet, Mars, have to wear oxygen masks?”

“No,” said Hannah, firmly.

“So, you want me to begin from the beginning of oxygen masks?” asked Daniela, as was her name.

“Yes, and why it became a necessity to live there,” answered Hannah.

As the story goes, it all started with the Coronavirus. It began in 2003 in a country called China, as an epidemic, addressed as 'SARS-COV'.

Later on, in 2019, apparently, a man went to a fish market in the province called Wuhan, again in China."

Dani stopped to drink a glass of water.

"How lucky that you get to study all of this!" said Hannah.

"More like 'unlucky'. The mechanical professors give us tests every weekend, and I think if not sooner, later someone's head would crack under pressure!" Dani almost shouted.

"Please continue with the chapter," said Hannah.

"Alright, geek!"

Thus, in 2019, from a hospital in Wuhan, the new mutated coronavirus, called the 'SARS-COV-2' began to spread to other countries due to international travel.

Since then, what was called 'The Grand Clean-up' began, and billions of people were dying in only months.

In the middle of the year 2021, the Coronavirus had mutated three or four times, due to which even more people were dying.

In the past, because of population growth, billions of trees were chopped down for various purposes, such as making paper and furniture, so there was an oxygen crisis when the virus hit.

Millions of people were dying in a country called India. During that same period, many private companies such as SpaceX and Blue Origin, as well as NASA, worked together to create life-friendly conditions on Mars.

And right now, at this very moment, the 'Global Space Population Council' is striving to find and make life-friendly conditions on new planets."

Daniela completed the story.

But Hannah still had doubts.

"And what about the Corona Virus?"

"We will discuss that on the way to the holiday resort on Pluto, there is so much left to discuss!"

****

APPENDIX

Character Introduction

Ryan: Partially based on the author himself, he is the central character of the stories *Fish Keeper, Unexpected Gift*, and *Ryan left at Home*. Ryan is shown as a teenager who enjoys pets and technology and has a knack for fixing things, even damaged devices (as shown in unexpected gift, when he fixes the phone).

Meera: In the first chapter itself, she is introduced, but not named, until *Meera on the changadam*. In the third chapter, she is shown to be a mischievous, travel-loving girl who goes on to save her teacher and becomes the hero of the day after a ride through her village. However, it is *Ryan* left at home where she is finally introduced as *Ryan's* mother.

Lisa: In stories 1 & 2, *Lisa* is shown as *Ryan's* sister, a naughty girl who acts as the spark which starts a fight between herself and anyone. She is also a fish enthusiast and likes to play with her cousin, *Amy*.

Amy: In both stories 1 & 2, *Amy* is shown as the 'Lucky Girl', who gets something to herself, accidentally or not, every time *Ryan* visits her and his mother's village. In the first story, she becomes the proud owner of more than 200 fishes and a turtle, while in the second, she gets *Ryan's* maths textbook.

Shankar: *Shankar* is the protagonist of the story *The New Boss*. He is shown to be working for the company *Bio-Graphics*. In the story, *Shankar* is a biker who, one day, on the way to his workplace, accidentally brushes a man's car's mirror and gets in a fight with him, who later turns out to be *Shankar's* new boss, much to *Shankar's* misfortune.

Joshua Lewis: *Joshua Lewis* has an appearance in the story as *Shankar's* close friend who is excessively superstitious. However, it is in *The Believer* that *Joshua* is properly introduced to the readers as a superstitious middle-aged man, with the strange behaviour of always carrying around his superstitious and extreme devotion, which proves to be fatal, when he refuses help, claiming that 'God will save me!'

Will Jameson: *Will Jameson* is the central character of the story *Haunted House* and is shown as a teenager, who decides to go to the abandoned house in his neighbourhood, which is termed as a 'haunted house' by his friends. In the story, *Will* spends the night in the haunted house with his friend, *Andy*, and together they uncover a mystery, which leads to funny revelations.

Andy Wilson: *Andy* is introduced as a supporting character in *Haunted House,* in which he accompanies his friend, *Will,* to an abandoned house in their neighbourhood to win a bet. In *Broken Vase,* he is shown as a teenaged boy whose little siblings cause trouble for him, which all of them clear up together before their parents arrive.

Rajiv Krishna: A non-linked series of stories begins with *The Examination,* which has *Rajiv* as its central character. *Rajiv* is described as an average student, inconsistent with his studies, sometimes winning high marks, and sometimes falling below average. *Rajiv* resolves to earn high grades after becoming tired of always being inconsistent. The result is beneficial to him, yet ironically not very beneficial when he finds out that he learned the wrong subject on the wrong day.

The marigold flower: *The marigold flower* is the main character, acting as the parent of the titular character(s), the descendant marigolds. In the story, the marigold is shown as the most beautiful one among all others, which get plucked to be turned into a funeral bouquet along with other flowers, which finds its way to the funeral and gets disposed of in the garden, only to create a new marigold plant, from which more marigolds form. The marigold is symbolic to departed souls of our dears and nears.

Raman Rajeshwar: *Raman Rajeshwar* is the central character of *The Lost Ticket*, a man leading a middle-class life with his family. He has only a job that pays most of their expenses and repeatedly buys lottery tickets in hopes of becoming rich, despite getting reprimanded for his behaviour by everyone around him. However, he finally wins a crore in *The Lost Ticket'*, and goes on to run a travel agency, and own a large house, and live like a royal, as he desired.

Madhav: *Madhav* is the main character of the story *The Business Boy*. He is a business-minded teenager who rears fish as a hobby in addition to selling pet fish for a business. With the help of his classmates, *Madhav* eventually goes on to found a company that sells different kinds of pet fish.

Stephen Wilson: The protagonist of *The Death Wish* is *Stephen Wilson*. When the story opens, *Stephen* is depicted as a youngster, a desperate unemployed job-seeker, contemplating suicide, having no choice. However, *Tony*, a mysterious stranger who introduces himself as a robber, saves *Stephen*'s life and also entices *Stephen* into becoming a robber like himself.

Tony Jesper: The story *Death Wish* introduces us to *Tony,* the anti-hero, who saves *Stephen,* the protagonist, from taking his own life, while also offering him a job as a robber rather than staying unemployed and committing suicide. *Tony* is symbolic to the devil, in that he takes an innocent youngster, and turns him into an evil person, in this case, a robber.

Hannah Scott: *Hannah Scott* is the protagonist of '*When the Earth Was Still Green*', a teenager, who lives in the year 2037, when the human civilisation, and the species of every living creature that existed, has spread into space, mainly on *Mars.* With her curious mind, she becomes intrigued by the past of the planet from where all life originated, *Earth,* and so asks her sister to describe the history of human civilization to her.

Daniela Scott: *Daniela* is the second protagonist of the story *'When the Earth Was Still Green'*, who narrates the story of human civilisation, and why it spread out into space. According to the story, she is a college student and has a lot of knowledge regarding the evolution of various species.

REFERENCES

1. World Health Organization: Novel Corona Virus (2019-nCoV) Situation Report- 1; 21 January 2020, Data as reported by: 20 January 2020.

2. *The Wall Street Journal*- How it all started: China's Early Coronavirus Missteps; China's errors, dating back to the very first patients, were compounded by political leaders who dragged their feet to inform the public of the risks and to take decisive control measures: *Jeremy Page, Wenxin Fan and Natasha Khan;* March 6, 2020.

3. *News Feature*- 04 May 2020; Profile of a killer: the complex biology powering the coronavirus pandemic. Scientists are piecing together how SARS-CoV-2 operates, where it came from and what it might do next- but

pressing questions remain about the source of COVID-19: *David Cyranoski.*

4. *News Feature* 07 February 2020. Did pangolins spread the China coronavirus to people? Genetic sequences of viruses isolated from the scaly animals are 99% similar to that of the circulating virus- but the work is yet to be formally published. *David Cyranoski.*

5. *Microbiol. Aust. 2020* March 17: MA20013. Doi: 10.1071/MA20013 (Eupub ahead of print) PMCID: PMC7086482. PMID: 32226946. COVID 19: a novel zoonotic disease caused by a coronavirus from China: what we know and what we don't. *John S Mackenzie and David W Smith.*

6. MINI REVIEW article. Front. *Microbiol.*, 30 September2020.http://doi.org/10.3389/fmicb .2020.580137. The Potential Intermediate Hosts for SARS-CoV-2. Jie Zhao, Wei Cui and Bao-ping Tian. Department of Critical Care Medicine, The Second Affiliated Hospital, Zhejiang University School of Medicine, Hangzhou, China.

7. *IQ Air*: REPORT: COVID-19 impact on air quality in 10 major cities; last updated: 7/7/2021.

8. Positive effects of COVID-19 lockdown on air quality of industrial cities (Ankleshwar and Vapi) of Western India. *Ritwik Nigam, Kanvi Pandya, Alvarinho J Luis, Raja Sengupta and Mahender Kotha*. *Scientific Reports*, Volume 11: Article number- 4285 (2021) *Nature;* 19 February 2021.

AUTHOR BIO

Aman Paarthiv Krishnan is a 9th Grade student of Kendriya Vidyalaya NAD Aluva, Kerala. He is a student by day, an author by evening who writes simple, intriguing and real incident-based stories, and is the author of **Blossoming Souls**, his first book. He is a bookwormish student who started writing short stories at an early age of 10. He represented his school in the International Marrs Spelling Bee, and published a few stories in his school magazine. He is a lover of coffee, beaches and short stories, currently residing at Ernakulam.

He can be reached @ amanparthivsarath@gmail.com & you can visit his facebook page @ https://www.facebook.com/amanpaarthiv.krishnan

WhatsApp - +91 87926 36904

www.ingramcontent.com/pod-product-compliance
Ingram Content Group UK Ltd.
Pitfield, Milton Keynes, MK11 3LW, UK
UKHW021935190726
13853UKWH00004B/1459